HAPPY
HOUR

Thomas Ogren

ATTENTION READERS: We would like to hear what you think about our books. Please send your comments or suggestions to:

The Editors
Signal Hill Publications
P.O. Box 131
Syracuse, NY 13210-0131

This book is fiction. The author invented the names, people, places, and events. If any of them are like real places, events, or people (living or dead), it is by chance.

SIGNAL HILL

© 1990 Signal Hill Publications
A publishing imprint of Laubach Literacy International

10 9 8 7 6 5 4 3

ISBN 0-88336-218-X

Cover design by Chris Steenwerth
Illustrations by Cheri Bladholm

Signal Hill is a not-for-profit publisher. The proceeds from the sale of this book support the national and international programs of Laubach Literacy International.

 This book was printed on 100% recycled paper which contains 50% post-consumer waste.

To my parents, Quentin and Paula Ogren,
who taught me the love of reading,

to Betty Bradshaw,
who first encouraged me to write,

to Dan Kriger,
who suggested that I write this book,

to Sarah, Hildur, Naomi, and Joshua,

and, of course, to Yvonne,
the best wife a guy could have

Chapter 1

Eddie woke up on the hardwood floor. He was cold. His head ached. A loud sound kept playing in his ear. Voices. He was hearing loud voices. What were they saying? He couldn't make it out.

He shivered from the cold. All he was wearing was a pair of old Levis. His feet were bare, and his toes were cold. There was a foul taste in his mouth. "God!" he swore to himself. "Am I thirsty!"

He climbed up off the floor and stretched. His whole body was sore. Off in the living room, the TV was on. Some daytime soap opera was playing. The volume on the TV was way up loud.

Eddie stumbled into the living room and turned off the set. Well, at least it was quiet!

Too quiet. "Hey!" he yelled for the dog. "Hey, Choo-Choo! Come on, mutt!"

But the dog didn't come. Dumb dog!

Eddie walked to the bathroom. There were empty beer bottles all over the house. The place was a total mess. That wife of his! Some fine housekeeper she was!

And where was she, anyhow? And the boy— where was Jake?

Eddie stood in the bathroom and looked in the mirror. He looked as if he hadn't had a shave in a week. His eyes were red and bloodshot. The man staring back at him looked a lot older than 33.

Eddie used the toilet and then splashed water on his face in the sink. The face in the mirror seemed to be mocking him, calling him names. "Fool. Jerk. Lousy, drunken loser."

Eddie shook his head and walked to the kitchen. It was the worst of all. The sink was overflowing with dirty dishes. The trash can was turned over on the floor. Empty beer bottles and cans were everywhere. A plate with three half-eaten fried eggs sat on the table. A cigarette butt had been stuck dead center in one of the egg yolks. Flies buzzed all around the plate.

Eddie looked around for a full bottle of beer. There didn't seem to be any left. "To hell with it!" he swore. "I need a cup of hot coffee."

He found some instant coffee and put two spoons of it in a cup. He added some water and shoved it in the microwave oven.

While waiting for the coffee, he sat down at the dirty table. On the floor by his feet was a piece of paper. He picked it up and started reading.

"I'm sorry, Eddie," he read. It was a note from his wife. "I can't take it anymore. I'm gone for good this time. You can find a new wife or do what you like. I plan on getting a divorce. I can't live like this any longer. I'm going to stay with my parents up in the Bay Area. Please do not come and bother us. Jake will be better off without you. At least, he won't have to see his dad acting like a drunken fool all the time."

And that was all she wrote. Nothing more.

Eddie sat there for a long time. He forgot all about the coffee in the microwave. He forgot about everything for a while and fell asleep. When he awoke, a fly was buzzing in his face.

The note sat there on the table. Damn her! She was gone, all right. Annie wasn't one for making false threats—not anymore. They had already been through years of that. He had really blown it this time.

On the table next to an overflowing ashtray was a vase of flowers. It wasn't really a vase, just an old pickle jar. In it was a bunch of roses that Annie had picked, dried up now.

He had always meant to buy her a proper flower vase. But he never had.

The house seemed so quiet, so empty. He didn't like it at all.

How long had Annie and Jake been gone? Somehow, it seemed like a long, long time.

By now, they were probably all right—even happy. They were probably glad to be rid of him once and for all. Annie was still good-looking. She could find another man. A better man. One who didn't drink and tear up the house.

Eddie sat there for more than an hour. I ought to do everyone a favor, he thought. I ought to get my shotgun and shoot myself.

For a long time, he thought about this. No one would miss him much. No one depended on him anymore. Who would care if he was gone? And, for that matter, what would *he* be missing? Not much. His life was a lousy, stinking mess. He had no control over things any longer. Even his dog had left him!

Yeah, he thought, I should shoot myself.

But he just sat there. At last, he walked to the window that overlooked the back yard. His yard was a mess, too, dried-up and brown. Next door at the Itos', everything was green.

Eddie looked out across his yard and shook his head. In the vegetable garden, the squash plants looked wilted and dry. Weeds grew everywhere. He hated weeds.

He looked back at the messy kitchen. Annie was gone, and she wasn't coming back.

"Oh, God!" he heard himself cry out. "How did I ever let things get like this?"

Chapter 2

Ten years before, at the age of 23, Eddie Moreno was tall and thin. His hair was thick and black, and his eyes were brown.

Most people who knew Eddie liked him. True, he did drink a little too much, they'd say. And he had been in trouble when he was younger. He'd been to jail or something. But Eddie was all right.

Eddie worked five days a week on a landscape crew. He liked to grow things. He was always planting flowers or tomatoes or something. He had a garden in the back yard of his mom's house. He lived there with his mother and his two brothers and two sisters. Eddie's father had died when Eddie was 18.

Eddie's best friend since the eighth grade was Lance Nelson. Lance had just come back home to southern California after four years in the navy.

Tonight, Lance and Eddie were going out together. Lance had met some new girl. And he had set Eddie up on a blind date with her girl friend.

Lance picked Eddie up just before dark. "We still have an hour before we get the girls," said Lance. "Feel like a few beers?"

"Sounds good to me," said Eddie. So they stopped off at a bar on the way to pick up the girls.

It was "happy hour" at the bar. All drinks were half price. The bar was crowded with people. Rock and roll music blasted from the jukebox. People were laughing. There was free popcorn at the bar. And the beer was cold and fresh.

"There are some mighty foxy girls here," said Lance.

"Yeah, there are," said Eddie. "But how about this girl you got for me? You've never seen her?"

"No, I sure haven't, Eddie. But I expect she's nice. Suzy, the girl I met on the bus, she's a knockout. She said her friend's name is Annie. Annie Christino. Said she was tall, kind of thin, but real pretty. You'll like her."

"I suppose I will," said Eddie. "I just hope she likes me."

"Oh, she'll like you. What's not to like?" said Lance. "You think we've got time for one more pitcher of beer?"

"I don't think so, Lance. Anyhow, I don't want to go over there smelling like a keg."

"Don't worry about it, Eddie. You always worry too much. I'll tell you the truth. Women like the smell of beer on a guy's breath."

"You think so?" asked Eddie.

"Yeah," said Lance. "It turns them on."

Eddie took a long drink of his draft beer. It was good beer—fresh and cold. It tasted great. "Turns them on, huh?" he said.

"It always works for me," said Lance.

"Well," said Eddie, "I hope you're right. Let's hit the road. I'd like to stop off and buy some flowers."

"You don't need flowers," said Lance.

"I know," said Eddie. "But I'd like to get some. Maybe I'll get some roses. Yellow ones, if I can find them. Yellow roses for this Annie Christino."

"OK," said Lance. "Drink up. Let's do it!"

Chapter 3

"Roses!" said the girl. "I just love roses. How sweet of you."

Eddie felt himself blushing. He stood there and smiled.

Lance and Eddie took the two girls to a nice restaurant for dinner. All of them drank white wine with the meal except Annie. She said that she didn't drink.

Lance and Suzy ordered steaks. Annie said what she felt like was a chef's salad. Eddie was quite hungry, but he ordered a chef's salad for himself, too.

At the table, Annie was sitting on Eddie's right. As he ate, he tried to get a better look at her. She was tall, maybe five foot seven or eight. And her hair was dark, almost black. Her eyes were brown, he thought. He couldn't tell for sure, but he didn't want to stare. He ate his salad and sipped at his wine while Lance told stories about life in the navy.

Eddie noticed that Annie didn't touch any of the little slices of ham on her salad. She set them aside with her fork. "You don't eat meat?" he asked.

"No," she said. "I don't."

"I see," said Eddie. He took a long drink of his wine. The wine was cool and tasted good. He wished that this Annie would just drink a little bit. Girls who drank were always easier to talk to. If they drank a lot, they often did most of the talking for you.

"So," said Eddie. "Do you work or go to school?" He looked at her more closely. Her eyes were brown and quite large.

"I'm doing some of both," she said. "I'm taking classes at the junior college. And I work part time at a department store. What about you?"

Eddie told her that he was a landscaper.

"Really?" she said and smiled.

For the first time, it seemed he could see her clearly. She was thin, but athletic-looking. Her face was full of nice surprises. Her mouth, as she smiled, was very cute. "Landscaping," she said. "I'm impressed. I'm taking horticulture classes in college. I don't know much yet. But I like it."

"I had a horticulture class myself," said Eddie.

"Did you? Where?" she asked him.

Eddie decided to lie about this for now. "I had it in high school. But I took horticulture

14

for several years. It was my favorite class." He didn't tell her/he had taken the course/while he was doing time. She didn't need to know about that/right now.

Eddie looked at the bottle of wine on the table. It was almost empty. He wished that Lance would order another bottle. I could drink a whole bottle myself, he thought. Just slam it right down.

"Well," said Annie. "I think it's real neat—both of us liking plants. Most of the guys I meet are only interested in sports or cars. What kind of things do you do on your job?"

"We plant a lot of sod lawns," said Eddie. "And we build retaining walls. Plant shrubs and trees. Put in sprinkler systems. Lay out walkways. All that sort of stuff."

"I'm interested in all that," said Annie. "So what kind of job are you working on/right now?"

Eddie started to tell her about the new house/his crew was landscaping. Lance ordered another bottle of wine. Eddie, however, drank very little of it. By now, he was too busy thinking about Annie Christino. She was pretty neat, this girl.

After dinner, they left the restaurant and drove down to the beach. Lance and Suzy stayed in the car. Eddie and Annie took off their shoes and walked barefoot down the

15

beach. Eddie took her hand, and she didn't pull away. They walked and talked. She told him that she had three brothers and two sisters. He told her that his dad had died.

Annie told him that she wanted to get her own place. But everything cost so much. So she still lived at home. She and Suzy were thinking of getting an apartment together if they could save up enough money.

They talked about school and what they had liked and disliked. "My favorite thing was track," said Eddie. "I used to be pretty good in the mile."

"Hey," she said. "We ought to go running together sometime. I love to run."

"Yeah," said Eddie. "We ought to do that. I ought to quit smoking. I wonder if I can even run anymore."

"Let's see!" she laughed and started to run down the beach.

Eddie took out after her. His feet dug into the cool, damp sand. But she was quick, this girl. It was all he could do to catch up. Soon he was puffing hard. "I'm out of shape!" he gasped.

"I feel so good," said Annie. She wasn't breathing hard at all. "I feel like I could run for miles and miles."

"Well," gasped Eddie, "I hope you don't plan to."

16

"No," she laughed and slowed down and then stopped. "But I do love to run."

Eddie was still breathing hard as they walked back up the beach. A few years ago, he used to run six or seven miles easily. He decided that he was going to get back in shape. "You know," he told her, "I do work out, I lift weights. I never seem to get much bigger. But I'm pretty strong."

"You look all right to me," said Annie. "I like the way you're built."

"Yeah?" said Eddie.

"Sure," she said. "You look like a runner. Even if you don't run like one."

"You just wait and see," bragged Eddie. "I'll show you yet. I can run."

As they walked back toward the car, he held her hand again. Her hand felt warm and nice in his hand. Up in the sky, millions of stars twinkled. "Just look at those stars!" he said.

"Yes," said Annie. "It's a beautiful night, isn't it?"

"The best," said Eddie.

Chapter 4

Lance never went out with Suzy again. For Lance, she was just one girl out of many.

But Eddie started to see Annie Christino often. They would get together and just talk. Sometimes, they went for a run.

Eddie did not stop smoking. He did start running again, though. The first few weeks were tough. But, little by little, it all came back to him. He could feel himself getting stronger each week that he trained.

As the months passed, Eddie spent more and more time after work with Annie. Often, Lance would phone him. "Let's go get hammered!" he would say.

Sometimes, Eddie would go out, and they'd get drunk. But more often, Eddie would say that he couldn't make it. "Got a date with Annie," he'd tell Lance.

"You're spending too much time with her," Lance told him. "I was never all that impressed with her myself. Oh, she's cute. But she isn't my idea of a lot of fun and laughs."

"Well, I like her," said Eddie. Annie was the best girl he had ever met. And Eddie knew it. She was smart and hard working. And he thought she was fun even if she didn't drink.

Finally, Eddie told her that he had been to prison.

"I stole a car when I was sixteen," he told her. "I got drunk and stole a car. I got caught and did six months in juvenile hall for that. When I was eighteen, I got a year in prison for slugging a cop."

"You slugged a policeman?" asked Annie. "That doesn't sound like you at all."

"It was a mistake," said Eddie. "Me and some guys were drinking. I was pretty drunk, I guess. Some other guys came by in a car, and a fight started. I was fighting some big guy, and the cops came. I didn't even know the cops were there. One of them grabbed me from behind. I got free and punched him right in the nose. I gave him a bloody nose."

"And was that worth a year in prison?" asked Annie.

"No," he said. "It wasn't worth it at all. It was just plain stupid. But I did my time. I learned one thing: I don't ever want to go to jail again. And I don't ever plan to, either. So, do you still want to go out with me?"

"Yes," said Annie. "I'll still go out with you, Eddie. And I appreciate your being honest with me. But I should be honest with you, too. Your drinking bothers me. It really does. I think you drink too much."

"I happen to like to drink," said Eddie. "It's no crime, you know."

"It's not good for you," she said.

"That's not true," said Eddie. "Beer is almost like a health drink. The yeast in it is full of vitamins. And everyone knows that red wine is good for the blood."

"I don't know where you get your facts," said Annie. "Sounds like you've been reading liquor ads."

"You don't understand," said Eddie, "because you don't drink. You ought to try it sometime. You might like it."

"I can live without it," said Annie.

"I know you can," said Eddie. "But after a hard day's work, a couple of beers mellow you out. They help you relax. Say you go to a party, and you don't know anybody. You have a couple of drinks. You feel a little bolder. A little braver. Stronger. Funnier. Liquor makes things happen."

"I can make things happen without it," said Annie.

"Sure, you can, Annie. But you're missing out on something millions of people enjoy. Take wine, for example. Each kind of wine is made from different kinds of grapes with their own special flavor. The same is true for brandy and whiskey. Each one is different. Some are much finer than others. It takes years of work to produce a really fine wine or a good whiskey."

"I suppose that's true," said Annie. "I just choose not to drink. I feel that it isn't good for me. I don't want the extra calories. And I really don't care for the taste."

"Well," said Eddie, "a guy has to have a few vices. I work. I give money to my mother. I don't gamble, except maybe a few lottery tickets. But that's all. Nobody's perfect. Not even you, Annie. Although you do come close. So, are we going for that run tonight, or what?"

And they went for their run. Eddie was in good running shape now. They would often run five or six miles. They did this three or four nights a week.

Eddie kept up his drinking, too. Every day, he would have something to drink. But he no longer drank anything at all around Annie.

Before going to see Annie, he always shaved. He put on lots of aftershave lotion. He started to chew peppermint gum every day. It kept his breath fresher. It hid the smell of the booze, too. Or at least that was the plan.

The gum and the aftershave seemed to be working. Annie didn't bug him so often about his drinking.

One day at work, the foreman took him aside. "Eddie," he said, "I like your work. You stick to a job and get it done. You don't complain all the time. You don't do sloppy work, either. And that's hard to find anymore."

The foreman said that the company was starting a new work crew. How would Eddie like to run it?

Eddie said he'd like that just fine.

With his promotion to foreman came more work. He had to hire new men. The crews were expected to get a certain amount of work done each day. Men who didn't work hard made more work for the other men.

When a man didn't work hard enough, Eddie would warn him first. If that didn't work, he would fire him. Firing a man wasn't easy. But if you ran a crew, you had to be tough. The work had to get done right. And it had to get done on time.

There were good things about leading a crew. They would often start with just a new, bare house. The house sat alone on an empty lot.

Then they drew up plans. They dug ditches and laid in water lines. They put in sprinklers and planted trees. They planted shrubs around the foundation lines. They rolled out green sod lawns.

When they finished a job, it always felt good. Eddie would stand back from the house and look at it. He would admire the curve of the flower beds. He would notice the way the shrubs hid the harsh outline of the foundation. He'd look at the young, newly-planted trees. In 10 years, those trees would be 50 feet tall.

Eddie would stand there in the street, looking at the finished product. It doesn't look like just a house anymore, he would think. Now it looks like someone's home. And we made it look like that.

When they finished a job, he would let the crew off work a little early. And he would buy himself a bottle of good brandy to celebrate.

With the new job also came a big raise in pay. For once, he now had more money than he was spending. He started a savings account at a bank. Putting money in the bank was a good feeling. It felt like he was getting ahead.

Chapter 5

Annie finished her second year at the junior college. She went on to the state college, where she majored in horticulture. The more she learned about plants, the more she wanted to learn.

At school, Annie loved to work in the greenhouses. The air inside was moist and warm. Plants grew faster in the greenhouse. Seeds sprouted quicker. Flowers bloomed earlier.

"Someday," she told Eddie, "I want to have my own greenhouse. I'll grow plants and sell them for a living. It would be so much fun!"

"You could grow the plants," he said. "And I could plant them in landscapes. It's not a bad idea at all." Eddie was lost in thought for a minute. Then he spoke.

"We had a big greenhouse at the prison," he said. "In the winter, it was warm in there. Everything outside was frozen and brown. But inside we were growing tomatoes and strawberries and flowers—pansies, mostly. Our teacher was crazy about pansies."

Eddie went on. "It was pretty cool! The teacher used to let us play his radio in the greenhouse. We'd drink coffee. And we'd transplant plants from seed flats to six-packs. You'd forget you were in jail."

"You ought to visit the college," said Annie. "Come see the greenhouses. You'd like it there. You might even want to go to school there sometime."

"I never cared much for school," Eddie said. "I never did graduate from high school, remember?"

Annie said she knew that. But college was different. She loved college. Eddie would, too. He could start at a junior college even if he hadn't finished high school.

"Maybe someday," said Eddie. "But I'm making good money now. And I'm saving money. I like that. One of these days, I want to move out of my mom's place. I'd like to have a place of my own."

* * *

Eddie and Annie saw each other almost every day. One night, they were sitting in his car, parked by the beach.

"You know, Annie," he told her, "I sure like being with you. I like it better than anything else."

"I like being with you, too, Eddie," she said.

"You know that I love you," he said. "Will you marry me?"

"Marry you?" she said.

"Yes, marry me. Will you, Annie?"

She didn't say anything for a while. Eddie didn't know what to think. At last, Annie said, "I'd like to. I really would. I just don't know if we're right for each other."

"How can you say that? We get along great!"

"I know we do," Annie said. "But we don't like the same things."

"Of course, we do!" he cried. "We've got all kinds of things in common!"

"Yes and no," said Annie. "You see, I want the good things in life. I have a lot of ambition. I want to start my own business. I want a nice home. I want children, and—"

"Hey," said Eddie, "I want all those things, too."

"And I want a husband I can count on," said Annie.

"You don't think you can count on me, is that it?"

"I don't know, Eddie. You like to drink and have fun. We'd get married, and you'd get tired of it. You'd want to go out drinking with Lance. You'd want to have your wine, women, and song."

"I don't believe this!" said Eddie. "You've got me all wrong. I'm no big party kind of guy. I'd much rather be with you. I'll give up drinking if that's what you want. I won't touch another drop!"

"No," she said. "I don't want that. I don't want you blaming me because you're not having fun."

"OK," said Eddie, "so I won't give up drinking. I just won't drink very often."

"Mmm," Annie said, not sounding very sure.

"You know," said Eddie, "the worst time in my life was when my dad died. He had a heart attack. He was perfectly healthy, and then he died. None of us expected Dad to die. But he did. And I couldn't even go to the funeral because I was locked up. Oh, they would have let me go—in handcuffs. But I didn't want to put Mom through that."

Eddie went on. "I sure miss my dad. He and I used to fight all the time. But I miss him. We could have been such good friends."

Annie put her hand on Eddie's arm. "Getting married won't bring your father back," she said.

"I know that," said Eddie. "But I want what my mom and dad had. They loved each other. Maybe they never did get rich. Maybe they never took any trips around the world. But they had a good thing. They stayed together, and they enjoyed each other's company."

Eddie turned and looked into Annie's eyes. "Dad's death taught me a few things," he said. "We don't live forever. Life is short. Annie, if you don't want to get married now, I'll wait. I'll wait as long as I have to. But I want to live with you. I want to make big plans with you. I want to wake up in the morning with you next to me."

"Eddie," she said and laughed. "You argue so well. You ought to become a lawyer. Ask me again."

"Ask you again?" said Eddie. "Now?"

"Sure."

"Annie Christino, my love. Will you make me the happiest guy in the world? Will you marry me?"

"All right," she said. "Yes, Eddie Moreno, my love. I'll marry you."

Eddie laughed and pulled her to him. "That's what I wanted to hear," he said. "We're going to have so much fun together. Life is going to be great!"

"You'll have to ask my dad," said Annie. "You'll have to ask him for my hand in marriage."

"Isn't that kind of old-fashioned?" asked Eddie.

"Sure," she said. "But my father is an old-fashioned kind of man."

"What if he tells me no?" asked Eddie.

"He won't," said Annie. "Just ask him, all right?"

Chapter 6

The next day, Eddie went to visit Annie's father. Mr. Christino was a short, thin man. He never talked much, and Eddie didn't know him very well. The man liked to sit at the dining room table and read his newspaper.

Eddie sat down at the table with him. "Pretty interesting, huh?" said Eddie.

"What?" said Mr. Christino.

"The paper. The newspaper."

"Yes," said Annie's father. "You could say that. You read the paper?"

"Oh, sure," said Eddie. "I read it all the time."

"The sports page?" asked Mr. Christino.

"Yeah," said Eddie. "And the other parts, too. Look, sir, I'd like to ask you a question."

"So ask," said Mr. Christino.

"Annie and I would like to get married."

"Married?" said her father. "Married?" The man looked shocked.

"Right," said Eddie. "And if we could have your blessing, you know, your approval—"

"Hmm," said Mr. Christino. He shook out his newspaper and folded it. "Hmm," he said again.

"Well?" asked Eddie. "What do you think?"

"Do you love my daughter?" asked Mr. Christino.

"I sure do," said Eddie.

"And tell me, are you Catholic?"

"Yes, sir."

"Well, that's good. So you've already asked her?"

"Yes, I have," said Eddie. "And she wants to marry me."

"She doesn't *have* to get married, does she?" asked the man. He gave Eddie a long, hard look.

"No!" said Eddie. "Not at all. But we want to get married. If it's all right with you and Mrs. Christino."

Annie's father suddenly smiled. "Sure, I'll give you my blessing," he said. He shook Eddie's hand good and hard. "My Annie is a wonderful girl—and plenty smart. If she likes you, you must be OK. You're a lucky boy."

"Right," said Eddie. "I am."

* * *

The wedding date was set for the sixth of May. Everyone said that spring weddings were best.

Eddie asked Lance to be his best man. Annie asked her older sister to be her brides-

32

maid. Her little sister would be the flower girl.

Eddie's mother was overjoyed at the news. "That girl is a good catch," she said. "A fine girl. You'd better be good to her, Eddie."

"Of course, I will, Mom," said Eddie.

"I think I'm going to cry," said his mother. And with that, she broke into tears.

Eddie's mother got on the phone and called Annie's mother. They talked for more than an hour.

Annie, her mother, and Eddie's mother made a lot of plans. Getting married was a big deal.

Meanwhile, Eddie's life went on. There was more landscape work now than ever. A lot of new houses were being built. All of them needed landscape work. Eddie was working hard. Now that he was foreman, he liked to eat his lunch by himself. And he liked to have a few shots of whiskey each day at lunchtime.

But Eddie never drank in front of the other men on the job. He didn't want to set a bad example.

Sometimes, he would take a few quick drinks in the morning before work. Whiskey in the morning woke him up better than coffee, he thought. And then, after work, he would catch the happy hour at a bar near the job site.

But, he told himself, I'm going to have to cut back on the drinking. I'll soon be a married man.

And anyway, he told himself, I really don't need it. I can live without it if I have to. It's not like I'm some junkie.

And so, one day at work, he took only a quick pull on his pint bottle at lunch time. After work that night, he had only two fast beers at a bar. Two beers, he told himself. I'll become a conservative drinker.

The only thing was, it didn't feel like quite enough. It's crazy, Eddie thought. I always need things too much. I'm always too hungry and too thirsty. I can't give up smoking. But I'm going to have to back off the booze. I don't feel like it. But, by God, I will!

For several weeks, he stuck to his plan. Before going to work in the morning, he had just one quick little drink. No more. At lunch break, only one small pull on the bottle. After work each night, no more happy hour at the bars. Just two shots of whiskey. Just two shots and maybe one beer. But that was it! He was going to become a conservative drinker. He was going to learn to drink like a gentleman.

But it sure wasn't easy. It seemed as though he was used to more.

His body seemed to want—almost *demand*— a little more. It wasn't going to get it, though. He had everything under control now. He would have his couple of drinks. He would chew a little bit of peppermint gum. And everything would be cool.

Chapter 7

Eddie found a little house for rent. He took Annie with him to look it over.

The place needed paint. It needed plumbing work. It had been rented out for years and was kind of a mess. But the rent wasn't too high. And the back yard was huge. "It has potential," he told Annie.

"It has potential, all right," said Annie. "That's about all it has."

But they decided to rent it. "We can fix it up," said Eddie. "Even if we don't own it, we can make it a nice place to live."

"I'll paint all the rooms," said Annie. "I'll paint the walls white. That will make it seem bigger inside."

"And I'll landscape it," said Eddie. "I'll put in a sprinkler system and get the lawn to green up. We can make a little garden in back. Maybe we can even plant a few fruit trees."

"Oh!" laughed Annie. "It will be fun turning this little dump into a real home!"

Annie's parents and Eddie's mom gave them some used furniture. Several days before the wedding, Annie's brothers moved the furniture to the little rented house.

On May 6, Annie and Eddie were married. Just before the wedding, Eddie and Lance sneaked out into the parking lot. They had a few stiff drinks in Lance's car.

The wedding itself went well. The bride was beautiful. Everyone said that Eddie looked good, too. Women cried at the wedding. Men laughed and shook Eddie's hand.

The reception was held in Annie's family's big back yard. A small band played, and everyone danced and sang. There was plenty of food. Several kegs of beer were tapped. Many bottles of sparkling wine were opened.

Lance got so drunk that he got sick. He spent most of the reception passed out on a bed in the back room.

After the reception, Annie and Eddie drove to their little house. He picked her up in her long white wedding dress and carried her into the house. "Here we are!" said Eddie. "Home, sweet home."

The very first week, they started fixing up the house. They painted all the inside walls white. Annie made curtains for the windows. Eddie trimmed the bushes outside and started

digging a garden in back. They fixed broken light switches and leaky faucets.

They made great plans for the little house. As soon as they could afford it, they would paint the outside. Annie wanted blue with white trim. They would rebuild the fences and put in the sprinkler system. Maybe someday they'd be able to buy this little house.

In the meantime, they worked hard, loved each other, and enjoyed it all.

Out in the garage, Eddie set up his weights and weight bench. "I'm going to go out and lift," he would tell Annie. "I won't be too long." In a toolbox in the garage, he kept a bottle. He would have a couple of fast drinks from the bottle and then lift the weights a little.

Eddie always used lots of aftershave lotion to hide the smell of the liquor. And he chewed many sticks of peppermint gum. But still, sometimes Annie would smell it. "Have you been drinking?" she would ask.

"No," he would say most of the time. Other times, he would say, "Yeah, sure. I just had a little taste. It's no big deal."

"No big deal?" asked his wife.

"Right," said Eddie. "Let's not make a federal case out of it, OK?"

"OK, Eddie," Annie would say.

Chapter 8

Annie kept going to college. But, to save money, she cut back on her classes. And she started to work longer hours at the department store. They had been married almost three years when Annie got pregnant.

Eddie thought it was wonderful. "Maybe we didn't plan it now," he said, "but it will be great. Just think, a little baby of our own."

As the months passed, Annie got bigger and bigger. One night, she told Eddie, "I want you to quit drinking."

Eddie had just been out to the garage for a fast pull on the bottle. "Hey," he said, "I don't drink that much, honey."

"I don't care," said Annie. "No one should ever drink all by himself."

"So why don't you have a drink with me?"

"Right," said Annie. "That would be good for the baby, wouldn't it?"

"Oh, come on," said Eddie. "Can't you take a joke?"

"Not about this," said his wife. "I wonder if you shouldn't go to some AA meetings."

"Forget it," said Eddie. "I'm not a drunk. I can control my drinking. I just like to drink. Look, I go to work, don't I? You know, Annie, when I was in jail, I went to AA meetings. We had to do the whole AA thing there. And AA is great—for alcoholics. But I don't need it. It's a waste of time. And I don't have enough time for things as it is."

"Well," said Annie. "I don't know. We're going to have a baby soon. I don't want the baby to see you drinking all the time."

"I don't drink all the time!"

"Sure you do, Eddie. You drink all the time. You think I don't notice. But I do. I'm not stupid, you know. I just don't feel like pestering you all the time. I'm not your mother. And I'm not a cop, either."

"Yeah?" said Eddie. "Then don't act like one."

Annie looked down at her large belly and rubbed it without thinking. "I'm not saying you can never have a drink. I'm just saying, why not go to a few AA meetings? I know you drink almost every day. Maybe every day."

"I do not!" lied Eddie.

"Well, I don't know," said Annie. "But I don't like all the sneaking around."

"Sneaking around?" said Eddie. "Who's sneaking around?"

"You are!" said Annie. "You're always sneaking around. You're off to the garage to lift weights. You're down the street to get a hamburger. Or buy a pack of cigarettes. Or get some gas. You never buy a carton or fill the car up, just so you'll have an excuse to go out again real soon. I don't like it, Eddie. I don't like what it's doing to us. We never spend time together. We don't talk anymore."

Eddie stood there and shook his head. Pregnant women! Other men had warned him. Nothing was harder to live with than a pregnant woman. "You know," he said, "I think I'm a pretty decent husband. I don't gamble. I don't chase after other women. I stay home most nights."

"Yes, you do. But we don't share things the way we used to. We're not honest with each other."

"Do I lie to you?" he asked.

"In a way, you do," she said. "Those fast drinks out in the garage. Your quick trips to the bar or the liquor store. In a way, it's all lies. We weren't going to be like this, Eddie. And soon we'll have the baby. Why not just give AA another try. For me?"

"All right," said Eddie. "I'll quit the booze. I can do it. No problem, really. It's just a matter of a little will power. And I've got plenty of that."

"All right," she said. "Let's change the subject. What are we going to name the baby?"

They spent days talking about names for the baby. At last, they decided. If it was a girl, they would call her Naomi. If it was a boy, he would be called Jacob.

Eddie gave up his drinking.

All by himself, he did it.

He threw out all his half-filled bottles in the garage. He felt very proud of himself. He had it all figured out. Every time he had a craving for a drink, he would exercise. If he was out in the garage and wanted a drink, he would do three extra sets of the bench press. If he wanted a drink at work, he would do a couple of dozen pushups instead.

He would feel better, he told himself. He would look better, too. He'd lose his skinny look. He'd add pounds of rock-hard muscle.

One night, Lance came over with a case of beer. Eddie didn't drink a single can. Lance drank the whole case and passed out on their living room floor.

Day by day, Eddie lifted more weights. He started going for long runs in the evening. At work, he did pushups.

And all the time, he missed his alcohol. He missed it like a good friend who was no longer around. He missed that nice hot jolt of a shot of strong whiskey. He missed the laughter of the bar during happy hour. He missed the mellow flavor of deep red wine. He missed the malty taste and smell of ice-cold beer. He missed getting plastered.

He had expected to feel much better.

But he didn't. He didn't feel any better at all. In fact, he felt worse. He did seem to have more energy. But the energy had no direction. It led him nowhere. He felt himself getting short of temper, too. At work, he would catch himself yelling at his men over little things. At home, he would snap at Annie if the house wasn't clean. He'd yell if his favorite shirt wasn't washed. He'd get bent out of shape over the least little thing. And he couldn't seem to control his mouth anymore.

Some of us just do better with a little booze, he told himself. I'm one of those people. But I'll stay sober as a judge. I said that I would, and I will.

Life just isn't fun anymore, though, he thought. It really isn't. Without booze, nothing is really much fun.

One night, Lance told Eddie, "Since you've become a living saint, you're no fun anymore."

Annie didn't seem to value his new sobriety much, either. She was almost nine months pregnant now. Her belly was huge and hard and round like a big watermelon. Her back hurt her. She didn't sleep well.

One morning, Eddie was getting ready for work. Annie always put a pair of fresh socks and some clean underwear in the bathroom for him in the morning. Eddie got out of the shower and dried himself off. He sat down on the edge of the bathtub and put on his socks. One of the socks had a large hole in the toe.

"Hey, Annie!" he yelled. "These socks got holes in them. Didn't I tell you I hate wearing socks with holes in them? Do you have any idea what my feet feel like at work? Huh? Running around all day with my damn big toe rubbing against my work boots?"

No answer.

"Hey!" he yelled. "You listening to me?"

She opened the bathroom door. "Yes, I hear you. The whole neighborhood can hear you. Why don't you get another pair of socks? They're in your drawer. And why don't you quit yelling at me? You're always snapping at me now. Always finding fault with everything I do. I almost think it was better when you were drinking."

"Is that so?" yelled Eddie. "But I don't drink anymore, do I? I never touch a drop. I hope you're happy."

"Right," said Annie. "Living with you, how could I help but be happy!"

And with that, his wife went off to the bedroom and got back into bed. Eddie could hear her crying.

He took his watch from the counter and put it on. He checked the time. He was running late. No time for breakfast this morning.

Women! he thought. There's no pleasing them.

Chapter 9

Annie and Eddie had been going to natural childbirth classes at the hospital. She was learning how to control the pain of childbirth. Eddie was learning how to help her. The classes were fun. All the women were pregnant. A few of them did not have husbands and brought friends to help them. Annie felt sorry for them. Her own husband wasn't perfect, but he was hers.

On June 10, Annie's labor started. All night long, she could feel the pains, the contractions, getting closer. Early in the morning, she woke Eddie. "Call work," she said. "Tell them you won't be in. The contractions are getting close now. We'd better get to the hospital."

Eddie called his boss. The boss wished him good luck. They took Annie's suitcase and drove to the hospital.

Things went slow at first. And then it all hurried up. Annie was on the delivery table. Eddie was at her side. He coached her in how to breathe to control the pain, just the way they had learned in the childbirth classes.

Then the nurses told Annie, "Push. Push hard."

Eddie held her hand. She grasped his hand with a grip of iron. He wiped the sweat off her forehead. The muscles in her neck stood out clearly. He was surprised to see how much muscle she had.

"Push harder now," said the doctor. The doctor was a tall, red-haired woman. She was all business. "You're doing fine," said the doctor.

Then the baby started to come. Part of the head popped out. Eddie could see the baby's hair, dark and wet. My own baby, he thought.

Suddenly, the baby was out. "It's a boy!" said the doctor. "And a nice big one, too."

The baby boy started to cry. Eddie started to cry, also. The baby's crying was like magic music in the brightly lit delivery room.

Exhausted, Eddie drove home from the hospital. The house was too quiet. He was hungry and ate several sandwiches. A few beers would be nice right now, he thought. I could drink a toast to the new baby. But I don't drink anymore. Eddie ate another sandwich and went to bed.

After Annie and the baby came home, the whole place was different. There were now

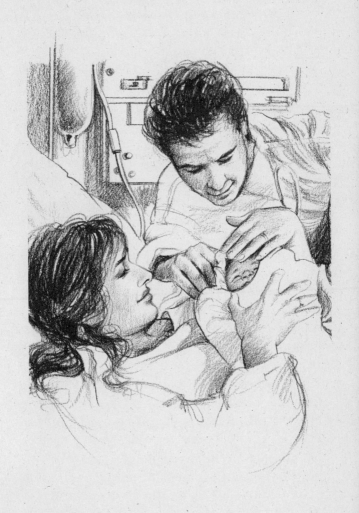

dirty diapers to change. And little Jacob cried at night when he was hungry. Annie nursed the baby. "It's better for him," she said. "It will make him stronger."

Sometimes, Eddie felt jealous of the baby. Annie would nurse him, and sing to him, and talk to him. Eddie felt left out.

One night, he was cleaning the garage. In some old boxes, he found a half-full bottle of brandy. Toss it out, his mind seemed to say. Oh, have a little taste, another part of him said.

"What the hell," he said to himself. "I'll just have a taste and then toss it out."

He took a little sip. It had that old bite that he remembered. That old flavor and smell. He took another sip of the brandy. Annie was busy with the baby. She wouldn't miss him. He sipped some more. Then he took a long drink. The old jolt was still there. It was just like old times.

He drank about half of the brandy and then hid it away in the box.

The next morning, he took a quick snort of brandy before going to work. Work seemed better that morning. At lunch, he drove to a liquor store and bought a fifth of vodka. He didn't like vodka as much as brandy or whiskey. But vodka was harder to smell on your breath. And it had that same good jolt. That nice little warm rush.

He broke the seal and took a couple of drinks. Work /after lunch/ seemed better, too. His whole mood seemed brighter.

After work, he hid the bottle of vodka with the brandy. Later that night, he polished off the rest of the brandy. "Well," he told himself, "I shouldn't be doing this. But I do feel better. I'll just have to be more careful. I've still got it under control."

And, for a few months, he did seem to have it under control. He drank every day. But he didn't get very drunk. And he didn't drink with Lance. "I'm still on the wagon," he lied to Lance.

"Suit yourself," said Lance. "Myself, I'm no saint. I enjoy a few drinks."

Chapter 10

Little Jake learned to crawl across the rug. Eddie would bounce him on his knee and talk to him. "We'll do lots of things together, Jakey," he'd tell him. "I'll take you to ball games. We'll go fishing. We'll go on long runs. Go camping. You and me, boy. We'll do it all."

One day on the way home from work, Eddie stopped off at a pet store. He bought a little golden-brown puppy for his boy.

"A boy should have a dog," he told Annie.

"All right," laughed Annie. "He'll probably chew up everything in the house. But he sure is cute."

The baby was crazy about the puppy. The puppy would run in circles around the baby and bark and bark.

"He's just like a little toy train," said Annie. "And he chews up everything in sight. Let's call him Choo-Choo."

"It's kind of a silly name for a dog," said Eddie.

"I know," said Annie. "But it fits him."

The puppy grew a lot faster than the baby. Before long, Choo-Choo was bigger than Jacob.

One day, the owner of the house dropped by. He was an old man. "You two have been good tenants," he told Eddie and Annie. "You keep the place nice and clean."

The old man offered to sell them the house. He didn't want to be bothered with it anymore. And the price he asked was low, too. It was a great chance for them to own their own home.

"If we can swing it, we'd love to buy the house," Eddie told the man. "I'll let you know."

Annie's parents loaned them the money for the down payment. But her father took Eddie aside. "How are things?" he asked Eddie.

"Just fine," Eddie said.

"You know," said Mr. Christino, "I think you drink too much, Ed."

"Why do you say that?" asked Eddie.

"I don't know," said Annie's father. "It's a feeling I have. Take my advice, son. Don't fall in love with the sauce. It will cause you nothing but trouble."

Eddie said he would remember that.

And, for a while, he tried to.

The tiny house was now theirs. Or at least it was theirs and the bank's. They were making payments every month.

Again, they made great plans for the house and their future. Soon Annie would graduate from college. She would try to get work at a big nursery. The pay would be better. She would learn the trade.

"I wish you would take some classes," she told Eddie.

"Maybe I'll do that," he said.

He didn't enroll in any classes, though. There was always too much work to get done.

Sometimes, he did think about college. But he couldn't see himself doing it. He drank too much and smoked too much. He'd been in jail. He was no college boy. And besides, there was no time.

And the time did pass quickly. Annie graduated from college. She found work at a big, new nursery.

Little Jake grew fast, too. He was walking and talking. He loved to chase the dog, Choo-Choo, around the yard.

Eddie started going to a bar near his house after work. Happy hour started just about the time his work was done for the day. Sometimes, he would stay too late. He would get too drunk. And then he couldn't get up for work in the morning.

Annie would call his boss. "Eddie can't make it to work today," she would say. "I think he's got a touch of the flu."

To Eddie, she said, "I think you're turning into a real drunk."

"Oh, give me a break," said Eddie. "I know what I'm doing. I don't drive drunk. I stay out of jail. I don't beat you."

"Don't even think about that!" she warned him. "You ever hit me, and I'll get my brothers to take care of you!"

"You're nuts!" he told her. And he got up and left the house. He went down to the local bar.

The little bar was a nice, quiet place. It was dark and peaceful. He could sit there at the bar and drink a few beers with the other guys. Maybe watch a little TV. Talk about sports. It was nice and relaxing.

Chapter 11

One day, Eddie was sitting at the kitchen table. It was a Saturday, and he was reading the newspaper. He smoked a cigarette and sipped at some black coffee.

He had already been out to the garage for his morning jolt of whiskey. Sometimes now, he drank in front of Annie. But he never did it in the morning. It wouldn't look right to her. It was too close to true alcoholic behavior.

Eddie put out his cigarette in an ashtray. Next to the ashtray was an old pickle jar that Annie used for a vase. There was a bunch of red roses in the pickle jar. The flowers were from the old Japanese couple who lived next door. The old couple were the Itos—Ted and Elsie Ito.

The Itos' house was small, but very clean. The paint was fresh, and their shrubs were always well trimmed. Their lawn was always lush and green. Ted Ito had a vegetable garden in his back yard. His vegetables grew like magic. His corn was tall. His tomatoes were big and red. His carrots grew to be a foot long and as thick as your wrist.

Eddie looked at the red roses. They reminded him of the Itos. For some reason, the Itos bugged him. Annie got along with them just fine. They were always giving her fruit from their trees or flowers from their rose bushes.

If I had that old fool's time and money, thought Eddie, my garden would be just as good as his.

At work, Eddie spent all day fixing up other people's yards. At home, he didn't seem to have the time, money, or energy to fix up his own. Old Ted Ito would always say hello to Eddie when he saw him in the yard. Eddie would nod his head. But he never talked to the man.

Eddie took another sip of his coffee. It was getting cold. He looked back to his newspaper and noticed the date. It was May 6. The sixth of May, he thought, and looked at the pickle jar of flowers. "Oh, right!" he said to himself. It was their anniversary today! Their eighth anniversary.

Eight years today! he thought. And I almost forgot, just like I did last year.

I know what I'll do, he decided. I won't say a thing all day. I'll pretend I forgot again.

Then I'll go downtown and buy her a decent flower vase. She won't have to use this old pickle jar anymore. I'll get her some flowers, too, he thought. A dozen yellow roses. Just like the ones on our very first date.

And then he'd give her the flowers and the vase and say, "Happy Anniversary, Annie. Get yourself dressed. We're going out to dinner." His mom would baby-sit Jacob for them.

Eddie got up and went out into the back yard. Jacob was playing tag with Choo-Choo the dog. "Hey, Jake!" yelled Eddie. "Where's that football of yours?"

"You want to play catch?" asked the boy. Jacob was tall for his age and skinny like his dad.

"Yeah," said Eddie. "Find your ball. Play a little catch with your old dad."

The boy ran off to look for his football. His dad hardly ever wanted to play catch. Dad must be feeling really good today.

They played catch for almost an hour. Jacob wasn't very good at catching a football. But as they played, he got a little better.

I should do this more often, Eddie thought. Dad never played much catch with me when I was a kid. Not like some boys' fathers did. And I was never that good at football, either. I won't let that happen with Jake. I'll start playing a little catch with him every day. Maybe just fifteen or twenty minutes. The kid is quick. He could turn out to be a good football player.

"Enough!" he told Jacob at last. "I've got to go downtown for a while. You go on in the house. See if Mom has got something for you to eat."

"Can I go with you, Dad?" asked the boy.

"No, I've got important things to do."

"Please, Dad?"

"No. Now, go and do what I told you."

Jacob went in the house, and Eddie went to the garage to get his car. He had a fast taste of whiskey, and it tasted mighty good. He was taking a second pull on the bottle when Jacob came into the garage.

"Hey!" yelled Eddie. "Didn't I tell you to go in the house?"

"I did go in the house, Dad."

"So go on," said Eddie as he tried to stash the bottle back in the toolbox. "Go on and play."

"Mom doesn't like you to drink," said the little boy.

"Listen, Jake," said Eddie. "Women don't know everything. You're a boy. Someday, you'll be a man, too. We men have to stick together. Don't go and tell Mom I was drinking in the garage."

"But you *are* drinking, Dad," said Jacob.

"So what?" said Eddie. "Don't be a fink. You're not a fink, are you? You're not a snitch, are you?"

"No," said his boy. "But Mom said the drinking is going to kill you, Dad. I don't want you to die."

"Oh, Jacob," said Eddie. "I'm not going to die. I'm just fine. Don't let women fill your head with all that crap. Men like to drink and fight and stuff like that. Women, girls—

they don't understand. So just don't say anything. All right?"

"OK, Dad." The little boy looked like he was going to cry.

"Look," said Eddie. "I've got to go now. Got to get something. I'll bring you back a candy bar if you keep quiet. OK?"

The boy nodded his head.

"In fact," said Eddie, "maybe we can play a little more football when I get back. Would you like that?"

"Sure, Dad," said his boy. "That would be super!"

Eddie drove downtown. He went in several stores. But he couldn't find just exactly the vase he wanted. He tried another store. They didn't have what he wanted, either.

There was a bar next to the last store. He had been in this bar many times before. It was called The Ring.

Eddie decided to stop in The Ring and have a quick beer. He had plenty of time, and he was thirsty. Real thirsty.

The Ring was a big, dark bar. The owner had been a professional wrestler 30 years ago. The owner's name was Hank. He often tended the bar. Eddie walked inside The Ring. It smelled good.

"Hey, Eddie!" said the big bartender. "How you been?"

"I've been all right, Hank," said Eddie. "Pour me a nice cold one, will you?"

"Coming right up," said the bartender.

Eddie sat down at the bar. This bar was one of his favorite places. The happy hour here was always packed with drinkers. It was early now, though. The place was quiet.

Across from the bar was a wall of mirrors. You could sit and drink at the bar. And you could look at yourself in the mirror. Dozens of bottles of whiskey, vodka, Scotch, brandy, and other liquors stood just in front of the mirrors.

Off in the back, some old rock and roll played from the jukebox. On all the walls of the bar were old photos of Hank back in his wrestling days. Hank was still a big guy. He weighed close to 300 pounds. "How's the beer?" he asked Eddie.

"Good," said Eddie. "Hits the spot. Let me buy you one, Hank."

"Well, I guess so," said Hank. And he poured a beer for himself.

"Hey," said Eddie. "The last time I was in here, some guy claimed you used to wrestle alligators. Is that true?"

"You bet!" said Hank. "Let me tell you about it."

"Do that," said Eddie.

Eddie sat there talking and drinking beer. Before he knew it, several hours had passed. More people came into The Ring. Happy hour had begun.

Hank turned up the volume on the juke-box. The beer flowed freely. Laughter filled the air. Several bar friends of Eddie's showed up. He bought a round for the bar. Everyone was having a grand time.

When closing time rolled around, Eddie was drunk. "Let me give you a ride home," said a man he knew.

"Naw," said Eddie. "I can drive."

"No, really," said the other man. "It's no problem. It's right on my way. And believe me, you're too drunk to drive."

"OK, partner," said Eddie. "Let's hit the road."

Eddie stumbled up the steps to his little house. It was dark inside. He got undressed and climbed into bed next to Annie. He reached over in the darkness and put his hand on her shoulder.

"Take your hand off me!" she said.

"Touchy, touchy!" said Eddie.

"Right," Annie said coldly. "And Happy Anniversary to you, Eddie."

"Damn!" said Eddie. "I knew I was forgetting something. Hey, I'm sorry, honey."

"You," said Annie, "can go to hell."

Chapter 12

Jacob went from kindergarten to first grade. Annie was promoted at work. She became sales manager at the big nursery. Annie's parents sold their house and moved up north to the Bay Area near San Francisco.

Sometimes, Annie would take a three-day weekend and drive up to visit her parents. She always took Jake along. Eddie always stayed home and got drunk all weekend.

Annie started going to Al-Anon meetings for families of alcoholics. She quit making excuses for Eddie. Now when he was too hung over to go to work, she wouldn't call the boss for him.

One day at work, Eddie's boss showed up at the job site. "Eddie," he said, "come on over here. I want to talk to you in private."

"What's up, boss?" asked Eddie.

"There have been some complaints about you," said his boss. "I take it you're still drinking."

"A little," said Eddie.

"A little too much," said his boss. "I think you ought to see about going to AA. I've seen AA do wonders for several guys I know."

"AA is for alcoholics," said Eddie.

"I know," said his boss. "That's why I'm suggesting it to you. You've been missing too much work. You know, I feel sorry for your poor wife. It must not be easy for her. So you think about that, all right?"

"OK," said Eddie. "I'll think about it."

"You do that," said his boss.

One Saturday morning, Annie and Eddie both slept late. Jake had spent the night at a friend's house. Annie and Eddie woke up at the same time.

"Good morning, little darling," said Eddie.

"Well," said Annie. "You're in a good mood for a change."

"I am," said Eddie. "Why don't you slip on over to my side of the bed? Now *that* would be something different."

"I wish I could," said Annie.

"There's nothing to stop you."

"Yes, there is."

"Won't you ever lighten up?" said Eddie.

"I wish I *could* lighten up, Eddie. But I'm not made that way."

"I know how you're made," he said. "You're made on the cool side. Damn cold, in fact."

"I'm getting tired of all this, too," Annie said. "Jacob is six years old now. You know I wanted to have another child. I've always wanted to have a little girl, too. But not now."

"Like I said before," said Eddie, "come on over here."

"No. No, I won't do it. I can still smell the booze on your breath. And that turns me off, if you want to know."

"Well," said Eddie. "I suppose I could get up and go brush my teeth if my breath offends you so much."

"That's just part of it, Eddie. I've been reading things in the papers. They've learned a lot about children of alcoholics."

"Uh-oh," said Eddie. "Here we go again."

"Right," said Annie. "And you ought to listen for a change. Children of alcoholics have plenty of problems. It doesn't matter if the drinking parent is the father or the mother. So far, Jake seems all right. But who knows how this will affect him later on? I want to have another child. But until you get sober, I wouldn't dream of having another baby with you. I won't even risk it."

"Have it your way," said Eddie. He got up out of bed. His throat was dry, and he was thirsty. Out in the garage was a bottle of relief.

That Monday at work, everything started to fall apart. A new man didn't get the work done the way Eddie wanted it done. "You!" Eddie yelled at him. "Get your stuff and split! You're fired!"

"Hey!" said another man on the crew. "You can't do that!"

"Sure, I can," said Eddie. "I'll fire all of you if I feel like it."

"We don't have to take this from you," said another man.

"Really," said the first man. "None of us like the way you've been running this crew. Always running your mouth off. You're a drunk. We're tired of taking all your crap."

"You!" said Eddie. "I already told you, you're fired. As for the rest of you, get back to work, or I'll can the lot of you!"

"You do that, big shot!" one of them said. All of the men picked up their things and left. Eddie was left alone on the job site.

Eddie tried to call his boss. The man was out, and Eddie left a message. He then drove to a bar and started drinking. He left at dinnertime and went home. He said nothing to Annie.

After a while, the phone rang. Eddie jumped up and grabbed it.

It was his boss. "I heard what happened," he said. "You've really messed me up this time! Tell you what, Eddie. Consider yourself fired."

"Is that right?" said Eddie.

"That's right," said his boss. "You're a darn good landscaper. And you used to be a decent foreman, too. But not when you're drinking. You get to AA. And when you've been sober for a month, give me a call. Maybe I'll still have a job for you. You got that?"

"Yeah," said Eddie. And he hung up the phone.

"What's the matter?" Annie asked him.

He didn't answer her. He just shook his head and left the house. He walked down the street and kept walking to the bar. Inside, it was dark and quiet. Eddie sat down at the bar and ordered a beer. "How's it going?" said the man on the barstool next to him.

"OK," said Eddie.

"You play the lottery?" asked the man.

"Sometimes," said Eddie.

"Me, too. I had a dream once where I won it. I believe in that. I don't know when. But I'm going to win the lottery."

"Is that so?" said Eddie. He wished the man would buzz off.

"You're darn right. I'm going to win the big one. Know what I'm going to do then?"

"No, what?" asked Eddie.

"I don't know," said Eddie.

"Or maybe because I'm so old?" asked Ted.

"No, Ted," said Eddie. "I just mean—well, I don't know. You always seem to have it so together. I've always been jealous, I guess. You and your wife, you're so happy together."

"Yes, we are," said Ted. And he smiled. "I'm a lucky man. Lucky to be alive. I used to be a big drinker. I drank all the time. I was drunk for years. I did terrible things. Stole stuff. Cheated people. Lied to everybody. Nobody trusted me. I was drunk for years and years."

"You don't drink now, do you?" asked Eddie.

"No," said Ted Ito. "No way!"

"So," said Eddie, "you got over it, huh?"

"No," said the old man. "You don't get over it. You never get over it. But I haven't had a drink in—well, about thirty years. Say, why don't you come over for a cup of tea? We can talk for a little while."

"I don't want to be a bother," said Eddie.

Ted Ito shook his head. "It's no bother. Elsie will be glad to meet you. And it will be nice to have some company. Come on over. We'll fix some tea."

Chapter 14

Eddie and Ted Ito talked for hours. They drank several pots of tea and made some sandwiches.

Ted Ito had been going to AA meetings for years and years. "I still go once in a while," he said. "I'm an old man. But I'm still an alcoholic. One or two drinks, and I'd be crazy again."

When Eddie was ready to go, Ted stopped him at the door. "You're still a young man," he said. "You like plants. Anyone who loves plants is good in his heart. Go to the meetings. Get off the juice. Everything will be all right."

"You really think so?" asked Eddie.

"Sure," said Ted. "You're not dead yet."

Eddie went back to his house. He thought about that. I'm not dead yet, he told himself.

He found the phone book and looked up the Itos' number. "Ted," he said. "Sorry to bother you. Would you mind going to an AA meeting with me?"

"Not at all," said Ted. "I could use a meeting myself."

Eddie spent the rest of the day cleaning up his house. He threw out beer bottles and washed dishes. He cleaned the toilet.

That evening, he and Ted went to an AA meeting. It was down by the train station. Eddie drove.

"You know," said Eddie. "As much drunk driving as I've done, it's a wonder I never smashed up my car."

"It's a wonder you never killed anybody," said Ted. "You've been lucky. Damn lucky."

The building where AA met looked old. A sign over the door said We Care.

Inside, on one wall, Eddie saw two large old photos. One was titled Dr. Bob. The other said Bill W. They were the men who had started AA. At AA, no one used their last names. After all, it was Alcoholics *Anonymous*.

A tall man came up to Ted, greeted him, and shook his hand. Ted introduced Eddie.

Then they got some coffee and took seats near the wall. All the chairs were placed in a big circle. One by one, people wandered into the room.

Up high on a wall, Eddie noticed a sign. It read One Step at a Time.

Eddie sipped his coffee and looked over all the walls. The Twelve Steps of AA were written on one wall. Next to them were the Twelve Traditions.

On another wall was a prayer. It started with the words *God grant me the serenity*. . . .

On every table was a bowl of hard candy. On one wall was a No Smoking sign. Under the sign was a stack of ashtrays. Half the people in the place were smoking.

Eddie looked around the room at the people. There were maybe 50 people in the room now. Some of them were old. Others were quite young. Some looked very poor. Others looked well off. Almost half of them were women.

The AA secretary called the meeting to order. He was a large man with thick red hair.

"Hi," said the secretary. "I'm Jack. I'm an alcoholic."

Eddie looked around the room again. Off in a corner, one man sat hunched over. He looked like a drunk. His hair was messed up, and he needed a shave. The man sat there, shivering in the warm room.

I know how you feel, thought Eddie.

The secretary talked to them for a few minutes. "I'm glad to be here," he said. "I'm fourteen months sober. Life is getting better all the time." He turned to the man next to him. "Pete, will you read?"

A man read them a selection from chapter 11 of the AA Blue Book. The chapter was called "A Vision for You."

Eddie's mind wandered. He looked up at the Twelve Steps on the wall. The first step said, "We admitted that we were powerless over alcohol—that our lives had become unmanageable."

Eddie thought about this first step. He *was* powerless over alcohol. No doubt about it. It controlled him. And his life had become unmanageable, all right. He had been doing a poor job of managing it.

The speaker asked if there were any visitors. Several people from other towns and other states spoke up. The secretary then asked if there were any people in their first week of being sober. Eddie raised his hand. "I'm Eddie," he said. "And I'm an alcoholic."

He had said this before, years ago in jail. But back then, he had never meant it. It was just a game then. It was no game now.

"Hi, Eddie!" everyone said to him. It felt good to hear them all say his name. He was among friends.

The secretary started people talking. He began with a man near him. "Hi. I'm Don. I'm an alcoholic," the man said.

"Hi, Don!" said all the people.

Don then told them that he had been a drunk for 10 years. He had been in and out of jail. He had smashed up several cars. His marriage had broken up. His kids wouldn't talk to him. But he had come to AA. He had started to talk to God. Things had gotten better. He had been sober for five years now. He was happy to be here, he said.

One person after another talked. A woman said that she had been sober now for seven months. Before that, life had been rotten. She had stopped drinking for several months on her own. But she was full of self-pity the whole time. No one could stand to be around her. With AA, she no longer felt sorry for herself. She was enjoying life again.

A very young girl talked. She looked no more than 18. She was a beautiful girl with long blond hair and large blue eyes. She looked quite unhappy. "Do I have to talk?" she asked.

"No," said the secretary. "You don't have to. But it would be good if you could."

"OK," she said. "My name is Toby. And I don't think I'm an alcoholic. But I got busted for being drunk in public. The judge sentenced me to go to five AA meetings. I started drinking when I was eleven or twelve," she said.

The girl said she had been in and out of jail. Her father always got her out. She had smashed up several of his cars while drinking. She had dropped out of school. Her life was a mess. She was crying as she talked.

Everyone listened. It was an amazing thing about AA meetings. When one person talked, everyone listened. No one interrupted.

As the young girl talked, Eddie wondered. How could she believe that she wasn't an alcoholic?

But then he hadn't thought that *he* was, either. But he *was* an alcoholic. And now he knew it once and for all. Thinking this, Eddie felt calmer. He felt peace come over him. Maybe he would be all right yet.

Several other people talked. One man was a lawyer. He had drunk for years. He'd been in every kind of trouble. He had made and lost fortunes. But he was sober now. And he was grateful to AA. "It saved my life," said the lawyer.

A woman near Eddie talked. "I used to drink all the time," she said. "And I was ruining my family. My little boy used to ride his trike near the swimming pool. I was in the house drinking. He could have drowned in that pool. I was just lucky he didn't. When my little girl was a baby, I would forget to change her diaper. Her little bottom would get all red and sore. I was so busy getting soused that I would just forget."

The woman looked across the room at the young girl. "All the drinking I did, Toby, I never went to jail. I never smashed up a car. I know *I'm* an alcoholic. If I were you, I'd have to wonder."

Suddenly, it was Eddie's turn to talk. "Hi," he said. "I'm Eddie. I'm an alcoholic. This is the first day in—I don't know—four or five years that I haven't had a drink." He told them how he got started. He told them what drinking had done to him. He talked for what seemed like a long time. And they all listened to him.

Afterward, a wooden bowl was passed around. Everyone put a dollar bill in it. Eddie put in his own dollar. It seemed like a real bargain.

At the end of the meeting, they all stood and held hands. They all said the Lord's Prayer out loud.

"Keep coming back," they all said. "It works."

87

Chapter 15

The AA meeting broke up. People came up to Eddie and talked to him. Several men gave him their phone numbers. They told him, "If you get in trouble, call us. If you feel like you just have to have a drink, give us a call."

As they drove home, Ted said to Eddie, "You know, you need a sponsor. Would you want me for your sponsor? After all, I live right next door."

"Sure, Ted," said Eddie. "I'd love to have you be my sponsor. Of course, I might turn out to be a lot of trouble."

"That's what we're here for, Eddie. We help ourselves by helping each other. That's the AA way of doing things. You do want to stop drinking, don't you?"

"Yeah," said Eddie. "I think I do."

"Then you'll do it. Nobody can stop for you. You have to do it yourself. But AA puts the power of the whole group behind you. We go to meetings. We help keep each other sober. And we ask God for help."

"I don't go to church much," said Eddie.

"That doesn't matter," said Ted. "God looks different to each of us. AA always talks about a Higher Power. We ask for His help."

Ted gave Eddie a copy of the Blue Book. "Look at chapter five," he said. "Read the Twelve Steps. Read them several times. Think about them."

"Those Twelve Steps," asked Eddie, "why are they so important?"

"They're a guide," said Ted. "The Twelve Steps are like a set of tools—tools to get and stay sober. You took the first step today. You admitted that you were a drunk. You admitted that you had no control over your life. That was the first step."

"OK," said Eddie. "I'll study the Twelve Steps."

"Right," said Ted. "Then get some sleep. And in the morning, water that poor garden of yours!"

Eddie read the book that night. He read it until he was tired. When he got in his bed, it felt empty. But he was sober. It was a start.

The next day, Eddie finished his cleaning. Then he went out to his garage and looked for bottles of whiskey. He found two he knew about and two he had forgotten.

Each bottle still held some whiskey. He took them outside. He opened each bottle and poured the liquor on the ground. The smell of the whiskey almost made him sick. Still, as he poured, he felt the urge to taste some of it. "Damn you!" he swore at the brown liquid.

He threw the empty bottles in the trash can. "Those," he said to himself, "will be the last liquor bottles I ever touch."

Ted Ito came over that day, and they talked. That night, Eddie went to an AA meeting by himself. That night, he slept alone again in his double bed.

The next day, Eddie started working on his garden. He attacked the weeds. One by one, he yanked them from the ground.

For the next two weeks, Eddie went to an Alcoholics Anonymous meeting every night. During the day, he worked on his yard. He got out his trenching shovel and started to dig. Ten years without sprinklers. It was long enough!

It took him several days of hard digging. But he dug all the water lines. He bought some PVC plastic pipe and sprinklers. He bought some automatic water valves and a watering clock.

When all the lines were in, he turned them on, one station at a time. He watched the sprinklers spraying water over his dry, brown lawn and garden. It looked great.

He was starting to run short of money. But he had a charge account at a hardware store. He bought several sacks of fertilizer. He spread the fertilizer carefully over the lawn. Now, he thought, I'll add some water. And then, watch this baby grow!

One day, he called his boss. "I just want to say—," said Eddie. "I just want to say that I'm sorry. Sorry I let you down like that."

"Are you going to AA?" asked his boss.

"Every day," said Eddie. "I haven't had a drink in two weeks now."

"Good," said his boss. "Let me know when you've been sober for a month."

At the hardware store, Eddie got some paint. For years, he had planned to paint the outside of their little house. Now, he painted it blue with white trim. Those were the colors that Annie had always wanted.

Annie, he found out, was still living with her parents up north in the Bay Area. Her boss had given her a long leave of absence. She often talked to Eddie's mother on the phone. But she never called Eddie. And he didn't call her.

He did start writing letters to his son. "Dear Jake," he wrote, "I just finished painting the house. It's blue and white. It looks like a new house. I miss you, son. Hope to see you soon. Love, Dad. P.S. Tell your mom I love her."

Every night, Eddie went to an AA meeting. Several times, he felt bummed out in the middle of the day. He then went to a daytime AA meeting.

There were AA meetings going on somewhere almost all the time. Drunks everywhere were getting free. And Eddie was, too.

When a sober month had passed, Eddie called his boss. "OK," said his boss. "Be at work tomorrow morning. We've got a lot of work to catch up on."

Eddie told all the men on the crew that he was sorry for running his mouth the way he had. They didn't seem happy to see him back. But they worked for him. And the work went smoothly. That night, he was tired. But it felt good to be working again.

One day, he stopped off at a nursery to buy some shrubs for work. He saw an apple tree called an Anna Apple. In this warm climate, it would bear two crops of apples a year. "Great trees," the salesman told him. "Good apples, too."

Eddie planted the Anna Apple tree in his back yard. His own Annie was gone. But maybe someday she would come back.

He heard from his mother that Annie had gotten a job up north. "I sure miss her," he told his mother. "I wish she would come home."

"Don't get your hopes up too much," said his mother.

"The next time you talk to her, why don't you suggest it?" said Eddie. "Tell her, 'Eddie sure misses you' or something like that."

"Well, Eddie," said his mother, "I'll tell you the truth. I don't blame Annie for leaving. What you put that girl through—it just wasn't right."

"I know, Mom," said Eddie. "But it was the booze that was messing me up. I'm sober now. Tell that to Annie when you talk to her. Tell her I'm not drinking. Will you do that, Mom?"

"All right," said his mother. "I'll tell her."

Chapter 16

Winter came. The days were cool. The nights were cold. Eddie went to AA meetings at night after work. He was a regular, and everyone knew him. He had been sober for four months now.

One by one, he was working his way through the Twelve Steps. He was now on Step Eight. He was making up a list of everyone he had hurt by his drinking.

It was a long list. The more he thought about it, the longer it grew.

His list included his wife, his son, his mom, his brothers and sisters, his boss, men who had worked for him. It went on and on. He had hurt plenty of people with his drinking.

It rained for three days in a row. At work, the crew worked in the mud. The rain made all the work harder.

One night, Lance came over with two six-packs of beer. They talked, and Lance drank. Eddie drank nothing but coffee.

Eddie thought of saying something to Lance. Like: Do you have to drink in front of me, Lance? Can't you see I'm trying to quit?

But Lance was his best friend. And Lance had always drunk beer, lots of beer. Lance never went anyplace without a 12-pack, at least. How was he going to ask Lance not to drink around him? Lance would get mad. And then he just wouldn't stop by anymore.

So Eddie said nothing.

Lance drank 10 cans of beer. When he left, there were still two full cans in the refrigerator.

Eddie threw out the empty beer cans. He cleaned up and went to bed. It was late, and he had to get up early for work tomorrow.

His bed felt cold and empty. If only Annie were here, he thought. I'd treat her nice this time. I'd be like a different husband. But she was gone. Maybe she had a new man by now.

At least, so far she had not divorced him. He dreaded getting a letter from her lawyer.

The clock by his bed ticked off the minutes. It was past one in the morning. Eddie was tired. But sleep wouldn't come.

If I drank just one of those beers in the refrigerator, he thought, I'd fall asleep fast.

Voices in his head spoke to him. They argued with each other. Oh, have one beer. No! Don't touch that stuff! You don't drink anymore. Oh, come on, relax. Have a beer. Just one lousy beer. It will help you sleep.

"I *am* thirsty," he heard himself say in the dark.

At last, he got up and went to the kitchen. He drew a big glass of cold water from the faucet and gulped it down. It helped some.

He looked at the refrigerator. He could picture the two cans of beer. They were his favorite brand, too. "Sit there and rot!" he yelled at them.

He went back to bed. Dumb thing to say, he thought. Beer in a can won't rot. He soon fell into a troubled sleep.

The next day, it was raining again. The soil had all turned to sticky mud. It was impossible to work. At lunchtime, he sent the men home.

On his way home, Eddie saw two young boys jumping in a big puddle. I wonder what Jake is doing today, he thought. I sure miss him.

At home, Eddie worked on a lawn mower out in the garage. At about five o'clock, he went in the house. The AA meeting started at seven.

He flipped on the TV. Some family show was on. A happy family with a mom and dad and three kids. They were all joking and laughing.

I feel like crap, Eddie thought. Sitting here all by myself. Working every day. And for what? Is this any way to live?

Down at the bar, happy hour was just starting. Drinks would be half price. People would be laughing, talking, doing a little drinking, and having some fun.

Eddie grabbed his jacket and left.

Inside the bar, loud music was playing. Eddie felt a powerful thirst building. He felt like a man who had been out in the desert with a hot, dry wind blowing on him. He could smell the beer in the warm air of the bar.

"Bartender," he said. "Pour this thirsty soul a long, cool draft."

Eddie sat on a bar stool and looked around. Some guys were playing pool. After a few more beers, he might join them. Off in a corner, three blond girls were chugging beers and laughing. Later on, maybe he'd try to pick up one of them. After all this time, he needed a woman.

He drank his beer and had another. And another. He made a trip to the rest room and had another beer. And another. He was counting them: six, seven, eight. Each one tasted better than the one before.

Eddie made another trip to the rest room. He drank more beers. New people came into the bar. Eddie paid them no attention. He was drinking hard. The beer tasted perfect.

He made another trip to the rest room and then bought himself another beer, number 15. He drank it down and asked for another.

His head was swimming. But Eddie felt good, very good. People were talking to him. He was telling jokes. Everyone thought he was funny tonight.

He polished off more glasses of beer. Number 20 was as smooth as number 1. He made another trip to the men's room and then bought another beer. His belly was feeling full. But he was still thirsty. He drank another beer. It still tasted good.

On beer number 27, he felt a sudden urge for fresh air.

"Going outside for some air," he told the drinker next to him.

Eddie staggered out the door. A cool wind was blowing. It felt good at first. He walked a few steps toward the street and felt ill. His gut knotted up tight.

A wave of cold swept over him. A force seemed to slam him hard in the belly.

"Ugggh!" he cried out in the dark. And up came the beer, up from his belly. Foul, stinking, second-hand, hot beer. It gushed out his mouth as he barfed into the street. He stood there like that for what felt like an hour. On and on and on, the 27 beers poured out of him.

Chapter 17

Eddie awoke cold and shivering. He was in his car. It was parked down the street from the bar.

It was still dark out. He looked at his watch. It was almost five in the morning.

He slapped himself in the face, hard, several times. He started up the car and drove home slowly. There are still two cans of beer in the refrigerator, he thought.

Eddie let himself into his dark, empty little house. A fine guy I am! he thought. Four months sober, and then drunk as a dog. Getting nowhere fast. He walked to his bedroom. He reached up to the shelf in his closet. There it was—the double-barreled shotgun.

In his dresser drawer, he found an old box of shells. He broke open the shotgun and stuck in two shells.

On his way to the back yard, he stopped in the kitchen. He opened the refrigerator and took out the two cans of cold beer.

Next door, Ted Ito was awake. He was an early riser. He was always out of bed by five in the morning. Ted was having toast and coffee when he heard Eddie's car pull up next door.

"Elsie," said Ted, "get me my shoes, will you? I'm going to go talk to Eddie. He must be in trouble."

Ted was just tying his shoes when they heard the first blast. Boom! Their kitchen window shook. And then again: boom! Ted jumped up from the chair. He ran out of the house with one shoe still untied.

Ted found Eddie in his back yard. The shotgun lay on the grass beside him.

"What are you doing, Eddie?" asked Ted.

Eddie was sitting there in the wet grass. "I shot them," he said. "The two beers. I blew them away."

In back yards nearby, dogs were barking. Lights were going on in houses.

"Come on, quick!" said Ted. "Get up off that grass! And give me that gun. Let's get over to my house before the police show up."

That day, Eddie and Ted went to an afternoon AA meeting. In the evening, Eddie went to another meeting by himself. "You're not the first guy to slide," people told him. "Just don't give up on yourself."

That night, Eddie slept over at his mother's house. "I just can't stand to be alone tonight," he told her.

In the morning, Eddie was back at work. The rain had stopped. The mud was starting to dry up.

After work that day, Eddie stopped off at the library. He checked out six books on landscaping. That night, he went to his AA meeting. After the meeting, he read the books. He read until he was tired and then went to sleep.

Two more months passed. Each week, he wrote a letter to Jake. Every two weeks, when he got his paycheck, Eddie sent part of it to Annie. With the money, he wrote a short note. "I figure you can use this. I miss you, Eddie."

By now, he had read all the books in the library on landscaping. He started reading the ones on horticulture. The more he read, the more he enjoyed it. Every night after his AA meeting, he would read until late.

In April, a man at an AA meeting told him about some land. The land was about 10 miles from his house. It was three acres of bare land. Nothing was on it but trash and weeds.

The man from AA introduced Eddie to the owner.

"I sure wish there was some way to rent that land from you," said Eddie. "I'd love to grow some nursery stock on it. But I don't have much money."

The owner said he planned to sell the land, but not for eight or nine years. Until then, it was just going to waste.

They struck a deal. Eddie could use the land. The owner would give him a year to get started. After that, he could pay rent. They agreed on an amount.

One weekend, his boss let him borrow the company tractor. Eddie mowed down all the weeds on the land. He picked up all the trash. Clean, the land looked much better.

In his mind, Eddie could see how it would look one day. Rows and rows of small shrubs would grow here. Sprinklers would water them.

"Ah!" he said to himself. "I'm going to do it."

* * *

On a Saturday morning, Eddie sat drinking coffee and reading the paper. He noticed the date, the second of May. Four more days until their anniversary on May 6.

There was something he had to do for this anniversary.

In an import-export store downtown, he found just the vase he wanted. He paid them to gift-wrap it for him. He took the vase to a florist shop. "Can you deliver it to the Bay Area?" he asked.

The florist said it could be done.

"Good," said Eddie. "I'd like to send the vase and a dozen of your best yellow roses. I'd like them to be delivered on the morning of the sixth."

"Do you want to include a note?" asked the florist.

"OK, sure," said Eddie. On a slip of paper, he wrote: "Annie, I just started building a greenhouse on land I leased. Wish you were here to give your expert advice. I need someone to go jogging with, too. Your sober husband, Eddie. P.S. Happy Anniversary."

Eddie paid the florist and drove out to his land. He started putting up the greenhouse. There was much work to be done.

Chapter 18

On the night of the sixth, Eddie's telephone rang. Could it be Annie? he thought.

He jumped up and got the phone. It was Lance. "What's going on?" asked Lance.

"Just sitting here, reading," said Eddie. "Hey, Lance, you know what day it is today?"

"No," said Lance. "What day is it?"

"My anniversary. Nine years since Annie and I got married," Eddie told him.

"How well I remember!" said Lance. "I had a terrible hangover after the reception. Why don't I bring over a case of beer? You and I can celebrate."

"There's not much to celebrate," said Eddie.

"Oh, I don't know," said Lance. "Maybe you're better off. That wife of yours—she was never any fun."

"Look," said Eddie. "I should have said this before, Lance. I should have said it a long time ago. Annie is still my wife. I love her. She's the mother of my son. You're always putting her down. I don't like it. I don't appreciate it."

"Oh, come on," said Lance. "Don't be so uptight. What you need is a good stiff drink."

"That's another thing I don't appreciate," said Eddie. "You know I'm trying to stay sober. I don't need the temptation. If you were a real friend, you wouldn't ask me to drink."

"I'm getting tired of your crap, Eddie," said Lance.

"Good," said Eddie. "Because I'm getting tired of yours, too." And Eddie slammed down the phone hard.

Eddie took out a cigarette and lit it up. His heart was pounding hard. So now he was done with Lance, too. His wife was gone. His son. His dog. His best friend. They were all gone.

He sat there and smoked. After a while, he picked his book up again. He would change what he could change. Things he couldn't change—well, he wouldn't worry about them. It didn't do any good.

He started reading again. The section on tree-grafting was very interesting.

He was just finishing the chapter when the doorbell rang. The sound startled him. The doorbell hadn't rung for a long time, not since Lance had last been over.

Well, thought Eddie. If Lance has a case of beer with him, I won't even let him in. I'm not putting up with it anymore.

He got up and walked to the door. Outside, a dog was barking. The dog's bark sounded like a bark he knew. The doorbell rang again.

Eddie opened the door. Choo-Choo jumped up and licked his face.

"I thought you'd never open the door," said Annie. She was holding Jake in her arms. He was sound asleep.

Eddie took the boy in his arms. "He looks older," said Eddie. "He looks like a little angel."

"That's because he's asleep," said Annie. "All the way down here, he was bugging me. 'Drive faster, Mom. Drive faster. I want to see Dad.'"

"Is that right? Did he say that?" asked Eddie. "I feel like crying."

"I know," said Annie. "I feel like crying, too." And, in fact, she was.

"Come here, honey," said Eddie.

Annie came up to him and hugged him.

They stood there crying and hugging each other. Jake, who was in the middle of them, slept through it all.

At last, they broke apart and laughed. They tucked their son into his own bed.

Eddie pulled the covers up over Jake and kissed him.

"When he wakes up, that is going to be one happy little boy," said Annie. "He sure has missed his dad."

"His dad has missed him," said Eddie. "He's missed you, too. It's good to see you, Annie."

"It's good to see you, too, Eddie. I loved the flowers—and especially the vase."

"Do you like it?" asked Eddie. "I was hoping you would. You won't have to use that old pickle jar anymore."

"No," said Annie, "I won't. As a matter of fact, I have the vase and flowers out in the car. Come on, Eddie. Help me bring all my stuff inside."

He took her hand, and they walked out to the car.

"The house looks great!" said Annie. "It looks like a new place. And you planted some new shrubs. And the lawn—we have a green lawn. Wow!"

"Right," said Eddie. "A lawn with sprinklers, too—automatic sprinklers, at that. It took me nine years to do it, but we've got sprinklers."

"I like it," said Annie. "I like it a lot."

They got her things and put them in the house.

"I'll bet you're tired," said Eddie. "Was it a long drive?"

"About eight hours," said Annie. "But I'm not too tired."

"Me, either," said Eddie. "I feel like having something to drink."

"You do?" asked Annie.

"Yeah," Eddie laughed. "I feel like having a cup of hot tea. How does that sound?"

"Sounds good," said Annie. "I never knew you to drink tea."

"It's something I picked up from the Itos," said Eddie. "I go over and have tea with them all the time."

"Really?" she asked.

"Sure," said Eddie. "Old Ted is a recovering alcoholic himself."

"Ted?" she said. "Ted is an alcoholic? I can't believe it!"

"I know," said Eddie. "But he used to be a big drinker. We go to AA meetings together. He's quite a guy."

They went into the kitchen, and Annie sat at the table while Eddie made a pot of tea.

"I like this," she said as she sipped the hot tea.

"The tea?" asked Eddie.

"Yes," she said. "The tea. The house. The yard. Just sitting here with you, Eddie. I like

it all. You know, you look as though you've gained some weight."

Eddie laughed. "I have," he said. "I've gained almost ten pounds. I've been eating better since I quit drinking. We're going to have to start running together again."

"That will be fun," said Annie. "Jake can go with us, too. He's been running with me. He's pretty fast."

"Hey," said Eddie. "I can't get over this—the two of us sitting here, sipping tea, talking. It sure is fun."

"We used to have fun," said Annie.

"I know," he said. "And we're going to have fun again, too. Lots of fun. Say, I've got to tell you about this land I leased—and my greenhouse."

"Tell me," she said. "Tell me all about it."

They drank two pots of tea. They talked for several hours. Eddie held her hand as they talked. Under the table, his foot rested next to hers.

"You know," said Eddie, "I think I had almost forgotten how pretty you are."

Annie smiled. "You think so, huh?"

"Yeah," he said. "You're the best thing I've ever seen."

"You're looking pretty good, too," said Annie. "I swear, you look five years younger."

"It's being off the booze," said Eddie. "This is the real me."

"I like the real you," she said. "You remind me of the guy I married—only better."

"Yeah?" said Eddie. "Say, it's getting kind of late. You tired?"

"No," said Annie. "Are you?"

"Not a bit," said Eddie. "You want to go to bed?"

"Sure," said Annie. "I'd like that."

Eddie jumped up from the table. "Hey," he laughed. "You remember when I asked you to marry me?"

"Sure," said Annie.

"I still remember it," said Eddie. "I told you that I wanted to live with you. I said I wanted to be able to wake up in the morning with you next to me."

"Tomorrow morning, my love," said Annie, "that's just where I'll be."

112

"First of all, I'm quitting my job. Who needs to work? Then, I'll buy myself a new car. Maybe a Rolls. And then—" The man kept talking. But Eddie wasn't listening.

This bar was full of dreamers. All the bars were. Big talk about the big score they were going to make. Talk about the women and the cars they were going to have.

Eddie drank by himself until the bar closed. Annie was awake when he got home.

"Well," she said. "Look at you now!"

"Go on to bed," said Eddie.

"Is something wrong, Eddie? Something worse than usual?"

"Go on!" he yelled at her. "Leave me alone!"

"You know," she said, "I've been going to Al-Anon meetings."

"Oh, give me a break," said Eddie.

"I have, Eddie. You're sick. Sick with drink. If you don't stop, it's going to ruin us. It's going to kill you. I can't go on like this. I want you to go to an AA meeting. Tomorrow."

"Maybe I don't feel like it," said Eddie.

"I'll leave it up to you," she said. "But I'm warning you for the last time. You get going to AA. And don't come in here all sloppy drunk ever again. If you do, I'm taking Jake, and I'm leaving."

"Is that so? You want to leave? So split! I don't need your constant nagging."

"I'm going to bed, Eddie. You sleep on the sofa. And remember what I said."

"Yeah, yeah," he said to her. But she was already on her way to bed.

He had a bottle in the garage. Half the night, he drank. He fell asleep out in the garage in an old stuffed chair.

In the morning, he left early so Annie would think he was going to work. He drank all day in one bar or another. "I figured out a new method," he told a bartender. "I just need to limit myself to two mixed drinks an hour. Either that or three beers an hour. And I think I can keep on drinking forever. I won't have to stop."

When the bars closed that night, he went home. He went straight to the garage. All night long he drank. In the morning, he left early again. He sat in a park and drank from a bottle in a paper bag.

When the bars opened, he hit them again. All day and into the night, he drank.

He left the last bar before closing time. He drove to a liquor store. The man there wouldn't sell him any liquor. "You're drunk," he told Eddie. "Go home and sleep it off."

"Take a hike, punk!" Eddie yelled at him.

He drove to another liquor store. There, he bought a half gallon of whiskey and three cases of beer.

"Going to do some serious partying, huh?" asked the clerk.

"You're damn right," said Eddie.

He drove home slowly. It was all he could do to keep the car on the road. His wife's car was gone from their driveway. "Must have gone to her parents," he told himself.

Eddie hauled his booze into the house and opened a bottle of beer. "It's happy hour!" he laughed. "Party time."

Eddie turned on the TV and started to drink his beer.

Chapter 13

Eddie woke up on the hardwood floor. He shivered from the cold. He was wearing nothing but a pair of old Levis. His feet were bare, and his toes were cold.

There was a foul taste in his mouth. His head ached. In fact, his whole body was sore. He climbed up off the floor and stretched. Off in the living room, the TV was blaring. Eddie stumbled into the living room and turned it off. At least it was quiet.

Too quiet. He called the dog. "Choo-Choo! Come on!"

But the dog didn't come. Dumb dog!

His bladder felt just about to burst. Eddie walked into the bathroom and used the toilet. There was what looked like old barf on the edge of the toilet bowl. Just the sight of it made his stomach feel weak.

He flushed the toilet and washed his hands. The man in the mirror had red bloodshot eyes. It looked like he hadn't shaved for a week. What a loser!

Eddie walked to the kitchen. The house was littered with empty beer bottles. The kitchen was the worst of all. The trash can was tipped over. Dirty dishes filled the sink. On the table was a plate of old fried eggs. A cigarette butt was stuck in one of them. Flies buzzed around the plate.

Where was his wife? And the boy—where was Jake?

Eddie looked around for a full bottle of beer. He gave up and made some instant coffee in the microwave instead. He sat down at the dirty table and waited for the coffee to heat.

On the floor, he noticed a piece of paper. He picked it up and read it.

"I'm sorry, Eddie," it said. "I can't take it anymore. I'm gone for good this time. You can find a new wife or do what you like. I plan on getting a divorce. I can't live like this any longer. I'm going to stay with my parents up in the Bay Area. Please do not come and bother us. Jake will be better off without you. At least, he won't have to see his dad acting like a drunken fool all the time."

And that was the whole letter from Annie.

Eddie sat there for a long time. He forgot about the coffee. Finally, he fell asleep. A fly buzzing in his face woke him up.

The note sat there on the table. Annie was gone. And so was Jake.

In the middle of the table sat a pickle jar. In the jar was a bunch of old dead roses.

The house was perfectly quiet. Empty. It gave him the creeps.

I ought to kill myself, he thought.

In his bedroom closet was a shotgun. He'd had the gun for years. He hardly ever used it. It was a double-barreled 12-gauge shotgun. It would do the job.

He thought about this. No one would miss him. There was no one he knew that he hadn't let down. So do it! he thought. Shoot yourself.

I'll do it, he decided. I'll do it today.

He got up from the table and walked to the window. The back yard was a mess. The lawn was brown. The garden was wilted and full of weeds. He hated weeds.

A fine yard for a landscaper! he thought. But then, he wasn't a landscaper anymore. He didn't even have a job. No job, no kid, no wife.

"Oh, God!" he cried out. "How did I ever let things get like this?"

Eddie went outside and sat on the back steps. He held his head in his hands. Tears ran down his cheeks. Real men don't cry, he thought. But what kind of man was he? He was no man. He was just a damn drunk.

Maybe there was something to drink out in the garage. That was it. He'd go have a drink or two. Then he'd shoot himself.

He got up from the steps and started toward the garage. I don't even have the class to die sober, he thought. "Hey!" he heard someone yell at him.

Eddie turned around. It was the old man next door. That damn old Ted Ito. Go away, old man! he thought. Eddie turned back toward the garage.

"Hey!" the old man called out again. "Say there!"

Eddie stopped and turned around. He looked at the old Japanese man. Well, there was no one else to talk to. Eddie walked over to the fence.

Ted Ito was short, thin, and very bald. He walked slowly to his side of the fence. "Hi, there," he said to Eddie.

Once Annie had asked Ted how old he was. "He's eighty-nine," she later told Eddie. "I think he's cute. Do you know what he told me? He said, 'I've lived a long time. I'm a lucky man.'"

"How are you doing?" Eddie said to the old man.

"OK," said Ted Ito. "So, things are not going too well?"

"Everything is all right," said Eddie. "Why do you ask?"

"Your garden," said Ted Ito. "It used to be so good. You always kept it watered." The old man shook his head. "Now, very dry. And lots of weeds. Lots of weeds for a long time. Things are no good, right?"

Eddie dropped his head. He felt funny all over. "No," he said. "Things are no good at all. My wife left me. Annie left. And she took Jake."

"I see," said the old man.

"I'm all messed up," said Eddie.

"You look OK," said Ted Ito. "Not great. But OK."

"I don't know, Mr. Ito," said Eddie.

"Call me Ted. You're Eddie, right?"

"That's me. Eddie Moreno."

"Nice to meet you, Eddie," said Ted Ito. He stuck his hand over the fence. Eddie took his hand and shook it. The old man's hand was thick and hard. Eddie hated to let go of it.

"I'm sorry I haven't been a decent neighbor," Eddie said. "I've lived here for almost ten years. And I've never even said hello. You must think I'm a real creep."

"Yes," said the old man. "I guess I have. Now and then."

"I'm sorry," said Eddie. "Really I am. I'm all messed up."

"What's the problem?" asked Ted Ito.

"I drink," said Eddie. "I drink way too much. I used to get mad at my dad. He didn't spend much time with me. So I drank. Then Dad died. So I drank even more. Or that was an excuse to."

"Yes," said Ted. "An excuse, all right. Drinkers always have a lot of excuses. I know. I'm an alcoholic myself."

"You?" said Eddie. "You're an alcoholic?"

"Sure," said Ted Ito. "You think Japanese don't drink?"